BTS : BANGTAN BOYS

SOUTH KOREAN BOY BAND

MR VIVEK KUMAR PANDEY

During Writing This Book No Character & No Religion Are Harmed . It's
Only For Entertainment & Study Purpose.

bts is kpop boy band from BigHit Entertainment.Bts means Bulletproof
Boyscoucts in korean but they have recently changes their english name to
Beyond the Scene.They have seven members (3 rappers and 4 vocalists) and
debuted on June 12th, 2013. Their fandom name is Army. Since then they've
accomplished many things. One of these things is that they have attended
the Billboard awards in America and won the Top Social Artist Awards.
BTS, also known as the Bangtan Boys, is a seven-member South Korean boy
band formed in Seoul in 2013.

Contents

Foreword

Author biography in English :

MY NAME IS VIVEK KUMAR PANDEY . I WAS BORN IN 30 SEP 2002,I AM FROM SURAT GUJARAT INDIA.MY DREAM WAS TO BE GOOD WRITERS ,MY FAMILY SUPPORTED ME TO SUCCESSFUL AND I CAN DO IT MY SELF.How do I write? That is a question, I believe, that can be honestly answered by me."CELEBRATING YOUNGEST WRITER AWARD WINNER IN GUJARAT 1ST RANK" MR PANDEY JI . I may think I did a good job writing something. The reader is the one who decides the quality of my writing. I do find writing to be natural to me and therefore find it to be a real challenge. My trick as a challenged writer is to do the best I can and know that I am happy with the final outcome. It may take a while to do my best and there may be quite a few problems I run into along the way.

I am not a greedy person those who are thinking about me and my self I never tried it anyone people suffering from sadness ,I trying to get promoted people suffering from happiness and joy in your Life Time. Now in current situation in India and also world people are unemployed and have no many but our indian governor help to people to get free food from ration card , i also take part in leadership team ,i am Motivational speaker , Film script writer. There was my two dream firstly writer and secondly actor & also my own film is upcoming soon i done almost completely completed script for my film .I AM GOING TO SAY WORD OF HEART TOUCH OUT PLEASE READ IT" , firstly i thanks my father he supports me in this field they always getting inspired me by own his words and behavior ,they always said that he was a biggest person in the world in future and also they purchase fruit and chocolate for me in anytime & anyway , firstly my father buy him then call me Vivek you want a chocolate i will say yes papa but how many tell me ,papa: you tell me how much i buy him i told 1 or 2 chocolate but my father purchase whole the boxes of chocolate and they get suprised me. MY FATHER WAS BORN IN " 20 SEPTEMBER" 1971 IN INDIA.

1) MY FATHER FAVORITE CLOTHES IS KURTA PAIJMA AND ALSO STYLES SHOE

2) FAVORITE SINGER IS KISHORE DA

3) FAVORITE STATE GUJARAT AND KOLKATA , HIS VILLAGE IN BIHAR

4) FAVORITE COLOR BLACK AND WHITE

THEY ALSO LOVE cricket like IPL and one day t-20 .they also like watching a News daily and heard the song daily ,they also interested in tik tok video but in current time tik tok is banned in india but also few videos are in you tube. In lockdown time my family and me very enjoy day daily. my father play daily ludo with his sister and son, daughter.they always loved tea and coffee anytime call me ". I make it tea for my father but some reason after the April to june they are suffering from fever and cough , weakness on 6 June 2020 my father death. they not told me say bye bye his life. After death of 6 June on 10 june my mom and dad anniversary.but my father is Best in the world they can do anything for me please take care of father and respect it of your parents.

ONE
BTS

- BTS

BTS (Korean Bangtan Sonyeondan), also known as the Bangtan Boys, is a South Korean boy band formed in 2010 and debuting in 2013 under Big Hit Entertainment. The septet—consisting of members Jin, Suga, J-Hope, RM, Jimin, V, and Jungkook—co-writes and co-produces much of their own material. Originally a hip hop group, their musical style has evolved to incorporate a wide range of genres; their lyrics have often discussed mental health, the troubles of school-age youth and coming of age, loss, the journey towards self-love, and individualism. Their work also frequently references literature, philosophy and psychological concepts, and includes an alternate universe storyline.

After launching in 2013 with their single album 2 Cool 4 Skool, BTS respectively released their first Korean-language studio album, Dark & Wild, and Japanese-language studio album, Wake Up, in 2014. The group's second Korean studio album, Wings (2016), was their first to sell one million copies in South Korea. By 2017, BTS had crossed into the global music market, leading the Korean wave into the United States and breaking several sales records. They became the first Korean ensemble to receive a Gold certification from the Recording Industry Association of America (RIAA) for their single "Mic Drop", as well as the first act from South Korea to top the Billboard 200 with their studio album Love Yourself: Tear (2018).

BTS became one of the few groups since the Beatles in 1966–1968 with four US number-one albums in less than two years, and Love Yourself: Answer (2018) was the first Korean album certified Platinum by the RIAA. In

2020, BTS became the first all-South Korean act to reach number one on the Billboard Hot 100 and Billboard Global 200 with their Grammy-nominated single "Dynamite". Their follow-up releases "Savage Love", "Life Goes On", "Butter", and "Permission to Dance" made them the quickest act to earn four US number-one singles since Justin Timberlake in 2006.

As of 2022, BTS is the best-selling artist in South Korean history, having sold in excess of 30 million albums via the Circle Chart, and their studio album Map of the Soul: 7 (2020) is the best-selling album of all time in South Korea. They are the first non-English-speaking and Asian act to hold sold-out concerts at Wembley Stadium and the Rose Bowl (Love Yourself World Tour in 2019), and were named the International Federation of the Phonographic Industry's (IFPI) Global Recording Artist of the Year for both 2020 and 2021.

The group's many accolades include multiple American Music Awards, Billboard Music Awards, Golden Disc Awards, and nominations for two Grammy Awards. In 2017, they partnered with UNICEF to establish the Love Myself anti-violence campaign, going on to address three sessions of the United Nations General Assembly. Featured on Time's international cover as "Next Generation Leaders" and dubbed the "Princes of Pop", BTS has also appeared on Time's lists of the 25 most influential people on the internet (2017–2019) and the 100 most influential people in the world (2019), and in 2018 became the youngest recipients of the Order of Cultural Merit from the President of South Korea for their contributions in spreading Korean culture and language.

· Name Of Bts

The septet's name, BTS, stands for the Korean phrase Bangtan Sonyeondan , literally meaning "Bulletproof Boy Scouts". According to member J-Hope, the name signifies the group's desire "to block out stereotypes, criticisms, and expectations that aim on adolescents like bullets". In Japan, they are known as Bōdan Shōnendan . In July 2017, BTS announced that their name would also stand for "Beyond the Scene" as part of their new brand identity.This extended their name to evoke those who grow up "from the boy to an adult who opens the doors that is facing to go forward".

· BTS in 2013 performing at the Incheon Music Center

BTS was formed in 2010, after Big Hit Entertainment CEO Bang Si-hyuk wanted to form a hip hop group around RM (Kim Namjoon), an underground rapper who was well known on the music scene in Seoul. BTS was originally supposed to be a hip hop group, but, seeing falling album sales, he changed his plans, thinking a different path would be more marketable. He chose to vary from the usual, highly regimented idol groups and create one where the members would be individuals rather than an ensemble, and free to express themselves. Auditions were held in 2010 with plans to original plans to launch the following year. The band members lived together, practicing up to 15 hours a day, and first performed before a small crowd of industry insiders in 2013.

We started to tell the stories that people wanted to hear and were ready to hear, stories that other people could not or would not tell. We said what other people were feeling—like pain, anxieties and worries. That was our goal, to create this empathy that people can relate to.

- BTS' representation by Big Hit

BTS' representation by Big Hit, rather than one of the three agencies that dominated K-pop at the time, allowed the individual members leeway to express their individuality and allowed them to have input into the music. On June 12, 2013, BTS released their debut single album 2 Cool 4 Skool, along with the lead single "No More Dream", neither of which sold particularly well at the time.

Nevertheless, according to Kathy Sprinkel in her book on BTS, that single was "spotlighting young people's anxiety in the face of lofty parental expectations, sent shock waves through the K-pop ranks. Here was a musical act that wasn't pulling any punches. More specifically, they had a point of view, and they weren't afraid to take on topics that are considered taboo in South Korean society and elsewhere." The album reached the top five on South Korea's Gaon Music Chart. In 2 Cool 4 Skool, BTS employed an old-school hip-hop sound from the 1990s. The album's release was followed by appearances on Korean music shows, which caught the attention of reviewers and viewers.

In September 2013, BTS released the second entry in their "school trilogy": the EP, O!RUL8,2?. The album was released alongside the single "N.O." Similarly to 2 Cool 4 Skool, the new release had a theme of students feeling under pressure and needing to sacrifice their dreams and aspirations. According to scholar Kyung Hyun Kim, many of BTS' earlier works such as "N.O." and "No More Dreams" were "expressions of rebellion against the establishment that tapped into Korean teenagers' frustrations with the country's educational system" and, he stated, helped them build a fan base among young people in North America and Europe. That same month, BTS starred in their own variety show, SBS MTV's Rookie King Channel Bangtan, in which members parodied variety shows such as VJ Special Forces and MasterChef Korea.At the end of the year, BTS was recognized with several New Artist of the Year awards in South Korea.

- Skool Luv Affair and first concert tour

The last entry in BTS "school trilogy", the Skool Luv Affair EP, was released in February 2014. The release topped the Gaon Album Chart, and appeared on Billboard's World Albums Chart for the first time, peaking at number three. The EP was supported by two singles: "Boy in Luv" and "Just One Day". Following Skool Luv Affair's release, BTS played at their first fan meeting in Seoul, selecting the name A.R.M.Y. for the fan club. In July 2014, BTS hosted a concert in West Hollywood, their first show in the United States, and in August, they appeared at KCON in Los Angeles.

In August 2014, BTS released the album Dark & Wild, which reached number two in South Korea. It was supported by two singles: "Danger" and "War of Hormone". The group embarked on their first concert tour, 2014 BTS Live Trilogy Episode II: The Red Bullet, which lasted from October to December 2014. The band launched their first Japanese studio album, Wake Up, in December 2014; the release peaked at number three on the Oricon Albums Chart. After the album's release, BTS held their 1st Japan Tour 2015 Wake Up: Open Your Eyes in February 2015. The Red Bullet Tour that had begun on October 17, 2014 in South Korea was resumed on June 6, 2015 in Malaysia and toured Australia, North America and Latin America before ending in Hong Kong that August. In all, the entire tour attracted 80,000 spectators at 18 cities in 13 countries.

- Bts success

BTS experimented with other styles of music besides hip hop in The Most Beautiful Moment in Life, Part 1, released in 2015.BTS wanted to express the beauty and anxiousness of youth and settled on the title of (Korean RR:

Hwayangyeonhwa), loosely interpreted to define "youth" metaphorically as "the most beautiful moment in life".

The album served as an introduction to their youth trilogy, a triptych of albums dedicated to the struggles of young people. The single "I Need U" was a top-five hit in South Korea and garnered the group a win on SBS MTV's The Show. The second single "Dope (Korean; RR: Jjeoreo)" reached number three on Billboard's World Digital Songs Sales Chart and its music video was viewed over 100 million times on YouTube. The group began the world tour extension of their Red Bullet Tour in June, titled 2015 Live Trilogy Episode II: The Red Bullet, visiting cities throughout Asia, Oceania, North America, and Latin America. "For You", in Japanese, was released together with Japanese versions of "War of Hormone" and "Let Me Know" on June 17, 2015, and immediately topped Oricon's daily chart.

· BTS performing at KCON France in Paris on June 2, 2016

In November, BTS commenced their third concert tour, 2015 BTS LIVE "The Most Beautiful Moment in Life: On Stage", which began with three sold-out shows in Seoul, and was extended to Japan. Thematically, the EP focused more on the serious and speculative aspects of youth, touching on the pursuit of success, loneliness, affection for their origins, and the suffering of the younger generation due to unfavorable conditions in current society. The album topped the weekly Gaon Album and Billboard World Albums charts. It also marked their first appearance on the Billboard 200 chart, making it for one week at number 171, and eight of the tracks appeared on Billboard's World Digital Songs Sales Chart.

Their compilation album and the finale to their "youth trilogy", The Most Beautiful Moment in Life: Young Forever was released on May 2, 2016. With 300,000 presold copies, it included three new singles: "Epilogue: Young Forever", "Fire", and "Save Me", which debuted in the top three spots on the Billboard World Digital Charts. The album topped Gaon Weekly Chart in South Korea for two consecutive weeks and reached number 107 on the Billboard 200. The Most Beautiful Moment in Life: Young Forever won Album of the Year at the 2016 Melon Music Awards. BTS embarked on their Asia tour extension, 2016 BTS LIVE "The Most Beautiful Moment in Life On Stage: Epilogue" from May to August 2016. Tickets for the 14 shows in 10 Asian cities sold out, some in as little as five seconds.

- BTS win Melon Music Awards

In September 2016, BTS released their second Japanese studio album Youth. The album sold 44,547 on the first day of its release, and charted 1ˢᵗ in the Oricon Daily Album Chart. The album was eventually certified Gold with sales of roughly over 100,000 in Japan.It was followed one month later in October, by their next studio album Wings, which combined the themes of youth presented in their previous "youth trilogy" with temptation and adversity. The album and its tracks, including the single "Blood Sweat & Tears" immediately rose to the top on eight music charts, including the Gaon Music Chart, and led the iTunes album charts in 23 countries. Wings opened at number 26 on the Billboard 200, with 16,000 album-equivalent units in the U.S. for the week of its release, the best week ever there for a K-pop album.It became the best-selling album in Gaon Album Chart history.

In February 2017, BTS released the repackaged edition of Wings entitled You Never Walk Alone. The 700,000 pre-orders of it (an increase from the 500,000 pre-orders of Wings) helped break the record for most albums sold in a month in South Korea, as it reached 1.49 million copies by the end of its first month. The lead single was "Spring Day" and it won Best Song of the Year at the 2017 Melon Music Awards. BTS' second world tour, 2017 BTS Live Trilogy Episode III: The Wings Tour, began in February.On the tour, BTS played arenas in the U.S., such as New Jersey's Prudential Center and California's Honda Center. Tickets for the North American leg sold out within hours and two shows were added. After completing the North American leg, BTS attended the 24ᵗʰ Billboard Music Awards in May and won Top Social Artist, the first K-pop group to win a Billboard award. BTS fans cast over 300 million votes for the band and broke a six-year winning streak held by Justin Bieber, a performer with 100 million Twitter followers. This caused the international media to focus on the ability of BTS' fandom to propel the group to such a victory.

BTS at their press conference in Seoul, South Korea after winning Top Social Artist at the 24ᵗʰ Billboard Music Awards on May 29, 2017

BTS released a remake of Seo Taiji's "Come Back Home" (1995) in July 2017, giving it new lyrics but maintaining the theme of urging societal change. Later that year, BTS embarked on their "Love Yourself" album series, with theme of the enlightenment of self-love through the (Korean ; RR: Giseungjeongyeol) narrative sequence of "beginning, development, turn, and conclusion." BTS released its first part, their fifth EP, Love Yourself: Her, on September 18. RM considered "DNA", the lead single from that album, as "taking BTS to new ground. We tried to apply new grammar and perspectives." He said of the album, "I believe it's going to be the starting point of a second chapter of our career; the beginning of our Chapter Two." Sonically, the EP served as "a dual exploration of the group's electro-pop and hip-hop leanings".

BTS at the 45th American Music Awards shortly before making a US television on November 19, 2017

Love Yourself: Her debuted at number seven on the Billboard 200. The album had 1,664,041 sales in May 2017 to lead the Gaon Chart, and was the first in 16 years to exceed 1.2 million copies sold since g.o.d's fourth album Chapter 4 (2001). "DNA" was released simultaneously with the EP, and its music video accumulated 21 million views in its first 24 hours. It became BTS's first entry on the Billboard Hot 100, charting at number 85, making them the first K-pop boy band to reach that chart. The single rose to number 67 the following week and became the highest-charting song on the Hot 100 for any K-pop group. A remix of "Mic Drop" from the album, featuring Desiigner, was released as a single and peaked at number 28, the first time a K-pop group had cracked the top forty. Both singles attained Gold certification from the Recording Industry Association of America (RIAA) in early 2018. "Mic Drop" achieved Platinum status in the US later that year.

In November 2017, BTS became the first K-pop group to perform at the American Music Awards. BTS won Artist of the Year at the 19th Mnet Asian Music Awards in December, winning for the second consecutive year. They released "DNA" and "Mic Drop" together with a new song "Crystal Snow" as a single album in Japan on December 6, 2017, though the songs were made digitally available elsewhere. It topped the Oricon Chart for the week of its release. It was the only album by a foreign artist to be certified Double Platinum in Japan in 2017.

Later that month, they made their Japanese television prime time music show debut on Music Station Super Live, and ended the year performing on Dick Clark's New Year's Rockin' Eve.

In 2017, BTS partnered with UNICEF on the "Love Myself" campaign, intended to help end violence, abuse and bullying, and to promote self-esteem and well-being among young people. Both Big Hit and the group pledged money to promote the campaign, and BTS sold special "Love Myself" merchandise and set up dedicated booths at concert venues. The campaign was renewed in 2021, with UNICEF deeming it to have been successful.

- Love Yourself album series

BTS won major awards at the Golden Disc and Seoul Music Awards in January 2018. In March, the group premiered an eight-episode documentary titled Burn the Stage that offered a behind-the-scenes look at their 2017 Wings Tour, exclusively on YouTube Premium. Their third Japanese studio album, Face Yourself, was released on April 4, 2018, and quickly reached the top 5 of the U.S iTunes Albums chart. A nine-minute short film, titled Euphoria: Theme of "Love Yourself: Wonder" and featuring the song "Euphoria", followed the next day as a prelude to the group's third Korean-language studio album, Love Yourself: Tear. BTS promoted Tear's May 18, 2018 release with an appearance at the 25th Billboard Music Awards two days later, where they made their initial BBMA performance with thei single, "Fake Love". The group also won Top Social Artist for a second consecutive time. The album coincided with the "turn" of the series, touching on the tortuous enlightenment of loving without being loved, the pains and sorrows of separation, and providing encouragement to those without dreams.

- BTS at their press conference for Love Yourself: Tear on May 24, 2018

Love Yourself: Tear debuted at number one its first week on the Billboard 200, becoming BTS' first number-one album in the US and the first K-pop album to top the US albums chart. It also became BTS' first top-10 release in Britain, reaching number eight on the UK Albums Chart. "Fake Love" became BTS' top-10 single on the Hot 100, the first time a song sung mostly in a language other than English had debuted in the top 10. BTS released their compilation album Love Yourself: Answer in August, 2018. The album was supported by the single "Idol" and its alternative digital release featuring Nicki Minaj.

Love Yourself: Answer sold over 1.9 million copies on the Gaon Album Chart in August 2018. The album became BTS' second number-one on the Billboard 200 and led to their highest US sales week in the country to that point with 185,000 album equivalent units.In November 2018, Love Yourself: Answer became the first Korean language album to be certified Gold by the RIAA. "Idol" and Love Yourself: Answer both received Platinum certifications in the US, with sales of more than 1 million.

In conjunction with Love Yourself: Answer's release in August 2018, BTS commenced their world tour, BTS World Tour: Love Yourself, with two concerts in the Seoul Olympic Stadium, which sold out in a matter of seconds, as did others of the 22 shows in 12 countries. In October, BTS released their collaboration with Steve Aoki "Waste It on Me", their first all-English language feature. For the final stop of the North American leg, the group performed at Citi Field in New York City, marking the first time a Korean act performed at a US stadium. According to StubHub, BTS was the second best-selling concert act outside the US, behind only Ed Sheeran. That October, BTS renewed their contract with Big Hit Entertainment through 2026.

In early November 2018, a popular Japanese music show cancelled BTS' performance, citing a T-shirt a member wore the year before, bearing a photograph of a mushroom cloud following the bombing of Nagasaki. In the same month, the Jewish human rights organization Simon Wiesenthal Center (SWC) stated that BTS owed an apology for that shirt, and for clothing and flags with Nazi symbolism. Big Hit Entertainment issued an apology, explaining that the images were not intended to be hurtful to the victims of Nazism or atomic bombings and that the group and management would take steps to prevent future mistakes. They also stated the flags were meant to be a commentary on the Korean school system. The apology was accepted by SWC and the Korean Atomic Bomb Victim Association. John Lie, in his scholarly article on BTS, opined that the Nazi incident showed that the group is not tightly controlled, as are other K-pop ensembles, whose every move seems scripted, and that the members have opinions and are not afraid to express them.

At the 20th Mnet Asian Music Awards, BTS won Artist of the Year and ranked number eight on Billboard's year-end Top Artist Chart and were also the number two act of the year in the Duo/Group ranking, only behind Imagine Dragons. They were also listed as one of the 50 most influential people by Bloomberg for their "willingness to address social issues, mental health, and politics, despite being in a genre often painted as bubble gum pop".

• Persona, stadium world tour and BTS World

In February 2019, BTS, for the first time, were presenters at the Grammy Awards. In April, Time named them one of the Time 100, the most influential people of 2019. Their EP, Map of the Soul: Persona, was released on April 12 with the single "Boy with Luv" (Korean; RR: Jageun geotdeureul wihan si), featuring American singer Halsey. The EP's release was followed by a performance on Saturday Night Live, the first K-pop act to appear there. Map of the Soul: Persona became the first Korean-language album to reach the number one position in both the UK and Australia, and the group's third album to top the Billboard 200 in less than a year. Map of the Soul: Persona became the best-selling album ever in South Korea in terms of physical copies sold, with more than 3.2 million sales in less than a month. "Boy with Luv" debuted at number eight on the Billboard Hot 100 in April 2019, the highest placement ever for a K-pop song.

- BTS performing at the Rose Bowl stadium in Pasadena, California before 60,000 fans

Following their two wins at the 26th Billboard Music Awards in May, including for Top Duo/Group, BTS embarked on their world tour stadium extension, Love Yourself: Speak Yourself. Due to the demand, BTS added more shows after tickets for the first dates sold out within two hours. In the lead up to the release of their mobile game BTS World, in June 2019 BTS released "Dream Glow" featuring Charli XCX, "A Brand New Day" with Zara Larsson, and "All Night" with Juice Wrld.

The group released the song "Heartbeat" with a music video from the game's official soundtrack, titled BTS World: Original Soundtrack. The soundtrack was certified Double Platinum by Gaon. On July 3, 2019, pre-orders for the single "Lights" crossed one million copies, marking the first time a foreign artist had accomplished this in Japan since Celine Dion in 1995. "Lights" debuted at number 81 on the Billboard Japan Hot 100 for the chart issue date of July 8, 2019 and reached number one the following week. On August 8, 2019, "Lights" received Million certification from the RIAJ, denoting shipments of one million copies.

Love Yourself: Her and Love Yourself: Tear both crossed 2 million copies in August. All three albums of the Love Yourself series have sold more than 2 million copies each in South Korea. Love Yourself: Tear gained silver certification by the BPI for sales in the UK, becoming their third album to do so following Love Yourself: Answer and Map of the Soul: Persona. For the final stop of their record-breaking Love Yourself: Speak Yourself World Tour, the group played Seoul's Olympic Stadium. BTS was the third top-grossing touring musical act of 2019. That same month, they released a remix version of the song "Make It Right" featuring Lauv. In November, BTS won three times at the 2019 American Music Awards, for Best Tour, Favorite Duo or Group – Pop/Rock, and Favorite Social Artist (the second consecutive year).

In December, they attended both the 2019 Melon Music Awards and 2019 Mnet Asian Music Awards. In each case, they became the first group to sweep the four major awards. At the 34th Golden Disc Awards, BTS became the first artists in history to win grand prizes in both the physical and digital categories in a single year.

Persona was named the second best-selling physical album of 2019 in the US by Nielsen Music behind Taylor Swift's Lover and was ranked sixth overall on the chart of Top 10 Albums (Total Sales) in the US. BTS wrapped 2019 as the fourth highest ranked group on Billboard's Top Billboard 200 Artists–Duo/Group ranking, behind Queen, Imagine Dragons and the Beatles. Map of the Soul: Persona was named as the third best-selling album of 2019 by the International Federation of the Phonographic Industry (IFPI), making BTS the first Korean artist to be listed on the Global Top 10 Album Chart in consecutive years. The IFPI named BTS as one of the best-selling artists of 2019 for a second consecutive year, making them the first non-English speaking act to achieve this.

• 7, "Dynamite" and Be

In January 2020, BTS released "Black Swan" along with a choreography art film performed by MN Dance Company of Slovenia as the first single from their album, Map of the Soul: 7. Album distributor Dreamus reported that stock pre-orders of the album reached a record-breaking 4.02 million. Later that month, BTS performed at the 62nd Annual Grammy Awards, making BTS the first Korean act to perform at the Grammys. Map of the Soul: 7 was released on February 21 to favorable reviews. The album was supported by the single "On" and an alternative digital release of it featuring Australian singer Sia. According to Gaon Chart, Map of the Soul: 7 sold over 4.1 million copies in nine days after its release, surpassing Map of the Soul: Persona to become the best-selling album in South Korean history and the first album to be certified quadruple million.

The album debuted atop the US Billboard 200, making BTS the fastest group to earn four number one albums since the Beatles in 1966–1968. "On" debuted at number four on the Billboard Hot 100, giving BTS its first top-five hit,, and the most Hot 100 top-10 entries of any Korean act, with three. BTS planned to support the Map of the Soul album series with a concert series, Map of the Soul Tour, beginning in April, but this was indefinitely postponed due to the COVID-19 pandemic.

In April 2020, BTS became the first K-pop artist to sell more than 20 million albums cumulatively, making them the best-selling artist in South Korean history. That month, amid the pandemic restrictions, BTS held a two-day online streaming concert event titled Bang Bang Con, where the group shared footage of past concerts on their YouTube channel. On June 7, BTS headlined YouTube's Dear Class of 2020 online graduation event, performing "Boy with Luv", "Spring Day", and "Mikrokosmos". Their commencement speeches highlighted their own graduations and offered "messages of hope and inspiration for the class of 2020 in both Korean and English". On June 14, BTS held an online live concert, Bang Bang Con: The Live, as part of the seventh anniversary of their debut.

It garnered peak viewership of 756,000 live viewers in 107 countries and territories, setting the record for the largest audience for a paid virtual concert. On June 19, BTS released the Japanese single, "Stay Gold", from their fourth Japanese album, Map of the Soul: 7 – The Journey, which was released worldwide on July 14. It surpassed 564,000 copies in its first week, breaking the record for highest first week album sales by male foreign artists in Japan.

BTS released their first English-language single, "Dynamite", on August 21. "Dynamite" debuted at number one on the US Billboard Hot 100 chart, earning BTS their first chart topper and making them the first all-South Korean act to earn a number one single in the US. The single also topped Billboard's new Global 200 for the week ending September 24, as well as Global Excluding US charts, becoming the first single to top both simultaneously. "Dynamite" peaked at number five on the US Mainstream Top 40 and on the. Billboard Pop Singles chart, becoming their first Top 10 on each and the former the highest-charting entry by a Korean act. On August 31, BTS made their MTV Video Music Awards (VMAs) debut with the first live performance of "Dynamite" and won four awards: Best Group, Best Choreography, Best Pop Video, and Best K-pop (the last three for their music video for "On"). On October 14, they performed the single at the 2020 Billboard Music Awards and won the Top Social Artist award for a fourth consecutive year.

On October 2, 2020, BTS released a remix of Jawsh 685 and Jason Derulo's single "Savage Love (Laxed – Siren Beat)". It topped the Billboard Hot 100 chart. On October 10 and 11, BTS hosted a two-day virtual pay-per-view concert, at KSPO Dome in Seoul, called Map of the Soul ON:E, which drew 993,000 viewers representing 191 countries or regions. On November 20, BTS released their fifth Korean studio album Be, with "Life Goes On" as its lead single. "Life Goes On" debuted at number one on the Billboard Hot 100 chart. With this, BTS achieved their third consecutive number one on the Hot 100 in three months. "Life Goes On" became the first song performed primarily in Korean to reach the top spot on that chart.

On November 24, 2020, BTS became the first Korean pop artists to be recognized by the Recording Academy when "Dynamite" received a nomination for Best Pop Duo/Group Performance at the 63rd Annual Grammy Awards. The group won the Special International Music Award at the 62nd Japan Record Awards.Kim, in his book on the influence of Korean popular culture, suggested that 2020, the worst year in many people's lives, was a noteworthy one for Korean culture, with Parasite winning the Academy Award for Best Picture, and BTS posting three number-one hits on the Billboard Global 200.

- BTS performing "Butter"

On March 4, 2021, the IFPI named BTS its Global Recording Artist of the Year for 2020, the first Asian and first non-English speaking act to top the ranking. BTS occupied three spots in the Global Album Sales Chart of 2020 with Map of the Soul: 7 coming in at number one, Be (Deluxe Edition) at number two, and Map of the Soul: 7–The Journey at number eight. In the newly launched Global Album All Format Chart, Map of the Soul: 7 claimed the first position and Be (Deluxe Edition) claimed the fourth position. On March 14, 2021, BTS performed "Dynamite" at the 63rd Annual Grammy Awards, becoming the first Korean nominee to perform, though they did not win the award. On April 1, BTS released "Film Out", the first single from their upcoming Japanese compilation album.BTS held a two-day online streaming event on their YouTube channel beginning April 17, titled Bang Bang Con 21, and aired three of their previous in-person concerts.

BTS released their second English-language single, "Butter", on May 21. The song debuted at number one on the Billboard Hot 100 chart—their fourth number one in nine months—making them the quickest act to achieve four number ones since Justin Timberlake in 2006 and the fastest group since the Jackson 5 in 1970. Their next English-language single,

"Permission to Dance", was released on July 9. It became BTS' eighth number-one on the Digital Songs chart, extending their record as the group with the most number-one entries on the ranking.

The band released the single "My Universe" with Coldplay on September 24, 2021. The single debuted at number one on the Billboard Hot 100, making it the first collaboration between two groups to debut at number one. The band held an online concert, titled Permission to Dance on Stage, on October 24, 2021, in Seoul. On November 23, "Butter" earned a Grammy nomination for Best Pop Duo/Group Performance at the 64th Annual Grammy Awards. Between November 27 and December 2, BTS held their first live performances before an in-person audience since before the pandemic. The band played four sold-out shows at SoFi Stadium in Los Angeles as a continuation of their Permission to Dance on Stage concert series.

On January 15, 2022, a fictional webtoon based on BTS, titled 7Fates: Chakho, was released. The comic surpassed 15 million views globally in its first two days of availability and became the highest-viewed title ever launched by Webtoon. The band held three limited-capacity concerts at Seoul Olympic Stadium on March 10, 12, and 13—the largest music gatherings approved by the South Korean government since the pandemic restrictions were imposed—with a total audience of 45,000 people.On April 3, BTS performed "Butter" at the 64th Annual Grammy Awards, though the song did not win the award it had been nominated for. On April 8, the band gained seven nominations at the 2022 Billboard Music Awards and won three, making them the most-nominated and the most-awarded group in the show's history.

BTS released their three-CD anthology album Proof on June 10, 2022. On June 14, during their ninth anniversary celebrations, the band announced a temporary suspension of group activities to focus on solo projects and other endeavors. Hybe Corporation, which owns Big Hit, clarified in subsequent statements that BTS was neither disbanding nor going on hiatus, but would be actively furthering their individual careers with the label's full support while still participating in future group activities, including the filming of Run BTS. The incident caused Hybe Corporation's stock to decline rapidly, resulting in a decrease in market value of $1.7 billion (US). On August 24, Billboard magazine reported that BTS would be performing in Busan as a group on October 15th in a benefit concert with all members participating under the banner of Yet To Come.

BTS member Jin (center) performing Freddie Mercury's "ay-oh" chant during their first concert at Wembley Stadium on June 1, 2019

BTS have cited Seo Taiji and Boys, Nas, Eminem, Kanye West, Drake, Post Malone, Charlie Puth, and Danger as musical inspirations. They have also cited Queen as an influence, saying they "grew up watching videos of Live Aid". During their concert at Wembley Stadium in London, Jin paid tribute to Queen by leading the crowd in a version of Freddie Mercury's "ay-oh" chant.

Their 2016 album Wings was inspired by Hermann Hesse's coming of age novel, Demian. Their song "Blood Sweat & Tears" quotes Friedrich Nietzsche's Thus Spoke Zarathustra, and its music video features visual references to Herbert James Draper's The Lament for Icarus, Pieter Bruegel's Landscape with the Fall of Icarus, and Pieter Bruegel's The Fall of the Rebel Angels. Among the literary and other sources that have inspired their works are those by Haruki Murakami, Ursula K Le Guin, Carl Jung, George Orwell and Nietzsche. The Love Yourself series was influenced by Erich Fromm's The Art of Loving, and their 2018 song "Magic Shop" from Love Yourself: Tear was inspired by James R. Doty's memoir Into the Magic Shop.

- Musical style

Since their inception, BTS have emphasized hip hop as their musical base, largely due to the influence of RM and Suga's background as underground rappers; during visits to the US, the group has received mentoring from American rappers. Bang Si-hyuk previously acknowledged that K-pop as a whole draws from black music, and author Crystal S. Anderson noted, "BTS's rising popularity in the US represents the continuation of the ways that K-pop functions as part of a global R&B tradition."

BTS experimented with R&B, rock and jazz hip hop on Dark & Wild in 2014; EDM in their The Most Beautiful Moment in Life album series moombahton and neo soul on Wings and You Never Walk Alone ; future bass, Latin pop in their Love Yourself album series Korean rap, electro disco, slow-dance ballads, emo rap, Afro pop, funk, trap, pop rock, and hip pop in their Map of the Soul album series; and disco pop in their single "Dynamite".

- Lyrical themes

Since their formation, BTS have believed that telling their own stories is the best way for the younger generation to relate to their music. Writing many of their own lyrics, the group discusses universal life experiences such as sadness and loneliness in their work and turn them into something lighter and more manageable. RM said that BTS tries to avoid a preaching or reprimanding tone in their songs "because that's not the way that we want to spread our message ... We're born with different lives, but you cannot choose some things. So we thought that love, the real meaning of it, starts with loving ourselves and accepting some ironies and some destinies that we have from the very start." When asked if it is difficult to write about things like mental health, Suga responded,

We feel that people who have the platform to talk about those things really should talk more, because they say depression is something where you go to the hospital and you're diagnosed, but you can't really know until the doctor talks to you ... More and more, I think artists or celebrities who have a voice should talk about these problems and bring it up to the surface.

Themes explored in BTS' discography have gone from exploring "the troubles and anxieties of school-age youth themes like love, friendship, loss, death, and more" Early BTS entries, such as "No More Dream" and "N.O" from their school trilogy, were described by Herman as motivated by personal experiences with South Korea's rigid approach to education and called for change to the educational system and societal expectations.The members' experiences with South Korean youth culture also inspired the songs "Dope" and "Silver Spoon" (Korean: RR: Baepsae) from their youth trilogy.

These songs reference generational disparity and millennials having to give up romantic relationships, marriage, children, proper employment, homes, and social life in the face of economic difficulties and societal ills while facing condemnation from the media and older generations. The group's label dubbed The Most Beautiful Moment in Life: Young Forever, the conclusion to their youth trilogy, "a special album that marks the conclusion of the epic journey of the series, containing the last stories told by young people who, despite an uncertain and insecure reality (The Most Beautiful Moment in Life Pt. 1) continue to surge forward (The Most Beautiful Moment in Life Pt. 2)." Wings focused on mental health, criticisms of the Korean-pop "idol" scene, and delivering a female-empowerment message.

The Love Yourself series introduced new themes regarding youth culture in South Korea, including the excitement of love, pain of farewell, and enlightenment of self-love. According to Sprinkel, BTS' 2020 "quarantine album" Be "chronicles the group's coming to terms with a suddenly new reality and offers support for their listeners going through the same upheaval and uncertainty".

BTS' lyrics have also addressed topics outside youth culture specifically. The song "Am I Wrong" from Wings questioned societal apathy towards changing the status quo; the lyric "We're all dogs and pigs / we become dogs because we're angry" appeared to reference South Korean Ministry of Education official Na Hyang-wook, who advocated a caste system for the country and who reportedly described average people as "dogs and pigs". BTS released the song amid the 2016 South Korean political scandal that resulted in the impeachment of president Park Geun-hye.

RM and Suga's personal struggles with mental health have inspired some of their music. "Not Today" from 2017's You Never Walk Alone is an anti-establishment anthem, urging "all the underdogs in the world" to keep fighting, and "Spring Day" honored the victims of the Sewol Ferry tragedy. Journalist Jeff Benjamin praised BTS in Fuse for "speak[ing] honestly about topics they deem important, even in a conservative society". Former South Korean president Moon Jae-in praised the septet: "Each of the seven members sings in a way that is true to himself and the life he wants to live. Their melody and lyrics transcend regional borders, language, culture, and institutions."

• BTS performing at the Korea-France

On April 29, 2019, Time magazine named BTS one of the 100 most influential people of the year, labeling them the "Princes of Pop". Billboard executive Silvio Pietroluongo stated the group was as influential as the Beatles.MRC Data executive Helena Kosinski noted that "although BTS weren't the first to open the doors to K-Pop worldwide, they were the first to become mainstream. They don't just appeal to young people but also to the 50s and 60s age demographic." The first non-English speaking artist to make the Global Artist Chart in 2018, BTS was the second best-selling artists worldwide across multiple media platforms, second only to Drake. In 2020, BTS became the first non-western and non-English speaking artist to be named IFPI's Global Recording Artist of the Year. In South Korea, BTS accounted for 41.9 percent of album sales in the first half of 2019, up from their market share of 25.3 percent the previous year.

In 2022, Youna Kim described BTS as having spearheaded the Korean wave, representing the global expansion of Korean culture as effectively as Psy did in the previous decade and with the strength of influence that the Academy Award-winning South Korean film Parasite had in 2020. South Korea's central bank, the Bank of Korea, found in 2021 that BTS, including a "ripple effect" that included increased tourism to South Korea; increased interest in Korean culture, movies, and study of the Korean language; and added approximately US$5 billion per year to South Korea's economy, a growth of about 0.5 percent. A 2018 study showed that, on average, 800,000 foreigners per year had visited South Korea over the past four years for BTS-related reasons.

Writers identified BTS as leaders even among other highly influential K-pop groups such as Girls' Generation, Super Junior, Exo, Twice, and Blackpink and note that BTS' success shows the importance of a strong, active fan base in the age of social media, where fan campaigning can be as important as musical quality to a song's success. The group has also distinguished themselves at the forefront of the business side of the K-pop industry by pursuing less restrictive contracts with their management company to maximize their artistic originality and creativity. With this newer approach to career management, BTS created closer ties to the South Korean youth and encourage individuality and authenticity among their audience.

- Diplomacy

Political scientist Joseph Nye developed the concept of soft power in his 2004 book, Soft Power: The Means to Success in World Politics,[which researchers such as Maud Quessard have applied to BTS and their influence on entertainment diplomacy and international relations. Nye wrote, "when one country gets other countries to want what it wants might be called co-optive or soft power in contrast with the hard or command power of ordering others to do what it wants". Youna Kim and Maud Quessard all read the currency of soft power as including culture, political values, and foreign policy, which applies to BTS' ability to be co-optive in their approach to spreading their message of harmony, acceptance, and addressing life's setbacks via their broad appeal on the international stage.

- BTS and President Joe Biden

Because of their influence, BTS were invited to address the United Nations General Assembly in September 2018 and perform before 400 officials, including Moon, at the 2018 Korea-France Friendship Concert in Paris, a summit celebrating the friendly relations between France and South Korea.

That year, BTS became the youngest recipients of the Order of Cultural Merit. Despite cultural medals traditionally being given to recipients with over 15 years of achievement, Moon recognized the group, five years into their career, for their contributions in spreading Korean culture and language worldwide. In September 2019, BTS were mentioned by Moon while announcing strategies for the content industries, for having pioneered innovative business models through direct communication with fans. In 2020, BTS were given the James A. Van Fleet Award in recognition of their outstanding contributions to the promotion of US-Korea relations, the youngest honorees to receive the award. In July 2021, they were appointed Special Presidential Envoy for Future Generations and Culture by President Moon. In their role as envoys, they help to "raise awareness on global agendas, such as sustainable development, to our future generations and to strengthen the nation's diplomatic power across the world" and appear at international events such as the 76th United Nations General Assembly. On May 31, 2022, BTS visited US President Joe Biden at the White House to discuss the recent rise in anti-Asian hate crimes and discrimination.

According to Kyung Hyun Kim, BTS' rise was facilitated by a great increase in music video programming and consumption on YouTube and the coming of an idol empire, including merchandising of nonmusical products, games, and fantasy fiction, as well as an expansion of online music fandom. The group has a large, highly organized, online community of fans, known as ARMY (Adorable Representative M.C. for Youth), which translates the group's lyrics and social media posts into other languages and matches charitable contributions of BTS' members. As of 2020, some 40 million ARMY members subscribe to the band's YouTube channel, with more than 30 million following the official BTS Twitter and Instagram accounts. The fan community helps generate BTS' number-one chart rankings via coordinated campaigns on streaming platforms, as well as pushes to feature BTS' music on radio stations and television. The demographic of BTS fans is overwhelmingly young and female, and some ARMY members may even surpass the group itself in influence.

Unlike other K-pop groups, BTS interacted with and engaged their followers from their earliest days over social media, as well as via BTS Universe, an alternate storyline involving the members told through music videos, mobile games, books, short films, and more that gives fans ample room to theorize. Kim suggested that ARMY are drawn to BTS since the members are seen as underdogs, originating from the Korean countryside and a relatively minor Korean entertainment company, which allows young fans to identify with them. BTS' lyrics speak to social values, and fans respond by trying to improve the world. As a result, the fandom regularly embraces activism on charitable causes and socio-political issues such as refugee crises, racial discrimination, children's rights, global warming, and the COVID-19 pandemic. Feedback from ARMY to BTS affects the group's actions and lyrics; BTS has eliminated certain Korean words that sound like American racial slurs from their songs and ended collaboration with a Japanese producer when Korean ARMY members deemed his views extreme.

Per South Korean author Jiyoung Lee, the relationship between BTS and ARMY is "a mutual exchange between artists and their fans" that is about more than merely "ensuring the band's primacy", but also "extending the band's message of positivity into the world". Lee opines that BTS and ARMY are "a symbol of change in zeitgeist, not just of generational change". The band members themselves agree and have long acknowledged their fans' role in their success. According to Sarah Keith, "BTS embody a moment of generational transformation. ARMY represents a 'coming of age' for the young, in which cultural production and influence are global and meaningful, and where the youth are politically and socially engaged."

- BTS Big Hit awards

Among BTS' endorsement deals, the group has partnered with Puma beginning in 2015, BTS initially promoted its sportswear as Puma Korea's brand ambassadors before expanding to become global ambassadors in 2018, and promoting the remix of Puma's "Turin" and "Sportstyle" line worldwide. In 2019, BTS signed with Fila to endorse its sportswear. BTS has also served as global brand ambassadors for LG Electronics' smartphones, and Hyundai Motors' 2019 flagship SUV the "Palisade" and hydrogen fuel cell electric SUV, the "Nexo". BTS became global ambassadors of the electric street racing series Formula E to promote how electric vehicles can help combat climate change. In 2020, BTS partnered with Samsung Electronics, releasing a limited BTS-themed version of the Galaxy S20+ and Galaxy Buds+. As the first male pop group ever to collaborate with Dior, BTS sported ensembles from Kim Jones' Pre-Fall 2019 collection at their concert at Stade de France. The band became global brand ambassadors for Louis Vuitton in April 2021

- Burn the Stage: The Movie

Burn the Stage: The Movie is a 2018 South Korean musical documentary film directed by Park Jun-soo and produced by Yoon Jiwon, featuring the behind-the-scenes of boy band BTS' 2017 The Wings Tour, an event known for drawing in more than half a million fans in 19 different countries around the world. It was released on 15 November 2018, and its distribution was handled by Trafalgar Releasing.

Tickets became available for pre-order on 22 October, and the movie was released in theaters on 15 November 2018, for a limited time at select theaters. The trailer for the film was released on 23 October 2018.

Due to popular demand it re-entered theaters in select countries on 5 and 6 December 2018. On its second run it beat One Direction's box office record for an event cinema release after reaching two million ticket sales.The film was released on YouTube Premium on 18 January 2019

TWO
PHILANTHROPY OF BTS

· *Philanthropy of BTS*

South Korean boy band BTS are known for their philanthropic endeavors. Multiple members of the band have been inducted into prestigious donation clubs, such as the UNICEF Honors Club and the Green Noble Club, in acknowledgement of the size and frequency of their donations. They have also received awards for their donations, with one member receiving a Patron of the Arts Award for donations to the arts, and BTS as a whole receiving a UNICEF Inspire Award for their Love Myself campaign. They often donate privately, with their patronage later being made public by the organizations they support and the media. The band's efforts have motivated their fans to also engage in various charitable and humanitarian activities, and on occasion even match their donations.

In 2015, BTS donated seven tons (7,187 kg) of rice to charity at the K-Star Road opening ceremony held in Apgujeong-dong. The following year they participated in ALLETS's "Let's Share the Heart" collaboration charity campaign with Naver to raise donations for LISA, a Korean medical charity which promotes organ and blood donation.

In January 2017, BTS and Big Hit Entertainment donated KR100 million (US$87,915) to the 4/16 Sewol Families for Truth and A Safer Society, an organization connected to the families of the 2014 Sinking of MV Sewol. Each member donated ₩10 million and Big Hit donated an additional 30 million. The donation was intended to have been made in secret. Later that year, BTS officially launched their Love Myself campaign, an initiative dedicated to funding several social programs to prevent violence against children and teens and to provide support for victims of violence in partnership with the Korean Committee for UNICEF.

• Other philanthropic ventures

In April 2018, BTS participated in Stevie Wonder's "Dream Still Lives" tribute to Martin Luther King Jr. That June, the band donated to the ALS hospital building fund. In September, BTS attended the United Nations 73rd General Assembly for the launch of the youth initiative "Youth 2030: The UN Youth Strategy" and its corresponding UNICEF campaign "Generation Unlimited". According to UNICEF, the goal of the initiative is "to provide quality education and training for young people". BTS were selected to attend due to their impact on youth culture through their music and social messages, previous philanthropic endeavors, and popularity among the 15-to-25-year-old age demographic.

Starbucks Korea partnered with BTS in January 2020, for their "Be the Brightest Stars" campaign that included limited-edition beverages, food, and merchandise exclusive to South Korea. A portion of the profits from the campaign went towards career and educational development programs for disadvantaged youth as part of The Beautiful Foundation's Opportunity Youth Independence Project.

Later that month, BTS participated in the Grammy week MusiCares charity auction event hosted by Julien's Auctions. The band autographed and submitted a set of seven microphones—the first-ever authorized items from them to be brought to auction—used between 2017 and 2019 during their Love Yourself World Tour. Initially estimated to raise between $10,000–20,000, the lot sold for $83,200, more than eight times its starting price and the highest of the event. All proceeds were donated to MusiCares, a non-profit organization that focuses on human service issues directly impacting the health and welfare of the music community.In June, BTS and Big Hit donated $1 million towards the Black Lives Matter movement, in the wake of George Floyd's murder; the band's fans matched the donation within 24 hours. The band later donated $1 million to Live Nation's Crew Nation campaign to support live music personnel during the COVID-19 pandemic.

With the continuation of the pandemic into 2021, BTS participated in another MusiCares fundraising auction held on January 29. The band donated a collection of outfits from their "Dynamite" music video that were projected to raise between $20,000–40,000. The ensembles auctioned for $162,500—over eight times original estimates—as the top-selling item of the event.

In March, the band became sponsors of UNICEF's global #ENDViolence campaign, and pledged to donate an additional $1 million by 2022. That same month, BTS donated seven outfits from their "Life Goes On" music video to the Grammy week charity auction hosted by Charitybuzz. Valued at $30,000, bidding took place from March 8–23, with proceeds going towards the non-profit Grammy Museum Foundation's music education initiatives. In October, the band contributed the custom Louis Vuitton suits worn for their "Dynamite" performance during the 2021 Grammy Awards, a set of rings worn by J-Hope for the same performance, and a signed Epiphone 56 Les Paul Pro electric guitar, to another MusiCares relief auction that was hosted by Julien's on January 30, 2022, as a precursor to the Grammy Awards in April. Estimated to raise between $30,000–50,000, the suits sold for $160,000, while the rings sold for over $24,000 collectively, and the guitar for $64,000.

· Logo for BTS' Love Myself anti-violence campaign

The Love Myself campaign was launched on November 1, 2017, in partnership with the Korean and Japanese committees for UNICEF. The idea was introduced by the group as a sponsorship to #ENDviolence, a global UNICEF campaign aimed at the protection of young people so they can live without the fear of violence, and promotes the hashtag #BTSLoveMyself, which asks fans and supporters to post self-loving photos with the hashtag to different social media platforms. With Love Myself, BTS became the first artist in South Korea to raise funds as part of a social fund for global campaigns.

In January 2018, BTS introduced donation platforms in collaboration with KakaoTalk as well as official stickers for the campaign. Five months later, in June, a partnership with the Japan Committee for UNICEF was announced through a partnership agreement ceremony held in Tokyo. BTS later attended the 73rd session of the United Nations General Assembly in New York on September 24, for the launch ceremony of UNICEF's global partnership, Generation Unlimited, a program "dedicated to increasing opportunities and investments for children and young people aged 10 to 24". On behalf of the group, BTS' leader RM delivered a six-minute speech in

English about self-acceptance and the Love Myself campaign.

In March 2021, BTS and Big Hit released a joint video statement with UNICEF and UNICEF Korea, announcing their renewed support of the campaign for two more years. The announcement also revealed that Love Myself had been "elevated to a multinational MCA partnership", marking the first time that a Korea-based partnership had been expanded to a "global trilateral partnership with UNICEF headquarters". The band pledged an additional $500,000 per year to UNICEF Korea. BTS also became sponsors of the global #ENDViolence campaign. They will donate a portion of income from their campaign merchandise and the "Love Yourself" album series sales to it, and a further $1 million to UNICEF Korea by 2022.Since its inception, the campaign has generated 5 million tweets and over 50 million engagements as of October 2021.

- Accolades

The Love Myself campaign won a UNICEF Inspire Award in the 'Best Integrated Campaigns and Events' category at the 2020 UNICEF Inspire Awards. Held annually by UNICEF Headquarters, the ceremony honours the "most innovative and inspiring" global UNICEF campaigns of the year across 18 categories. The 'Integrated Campaigns and Events' category awards campaigns that have generated the biggest influence and inspiration in areas including promoting children's rights, fundraising, and public relations. For the 2020 edition, 100 campaigns across 50 countries were considered, with winners selected through a combination of online votes by UNICEF employees worldwide and the evaluation of a judges' panel.

THREE
SUGA (RAPPER)

- *Suga (rapper)*

Min Yoon-gi (born March 9, 1993), known professionally by his stage names
Suga (stylized in all caps) and Agust D, is a South Korean rapper, songwriter
and record producer. Managed by Big Hit Music, he debuted as a member
of the South Korean boy band BTS in 2013. In 2016, he released his first solo
mixtape, Agust D. In 2018, he re-released the mixtape for digital purchase
and streaming. The reissue reached number three on Billboard's World
Albums Chart. In 2020, he released his second solo mixtape, D-2.
Commercially, the mixtape peaked at number 11 on the US Billboard 200,
number seven on the UK Albums Chart, and number two on Australia's
ARIA Album Chart. The Korea Music Copyright Association attributes over
100 songs to Suga as a songwriter and producer, including Suran's "Wine"
which peaked at number two on the Gaon Music Chart and won best Soul/
R&B track of the year at the 2017 Melon Music Awards.

- Suga life and education

Min Yoon-gi was born on March 9, 1993, in Daegu, South Korea. The
younger of two sons, he attended Taejeon Elementary School, Gwaneum
Middle School, and Apgujeong High School.

In March 2019, after graduating from the Global Cyber University with
a degree in Broadcasting and Entertainment, he enrolled at Hanyang Cyber
University for the Master of Business Administration program in
Advertising and Media.

- Suga Career

Suga became interested in rap after hearing "Ragga Muffin" by Stony Skunk, stating that it was different from anything he had ever heard before. After hearing Epik High, he decided to become a rapper.

By age 13, he began to write music lyrics and learned about MIDI. He worked a part-time job at a record studio by age 17. From then on, he began composing and arranging music, rapping, and performing. Before being signed, he was active under the name Gloss as an underground rapper. As part of the hip hop crew D-Town in 2010, he produced "518-062", a song commemorating the Gwangju Uprising.

- Suga performing

Originally joining the company as a music producer, Suga trained under Big Hit Entertainment for three years alongside members J-Hope and RM. He made his debut as a member of BTS on Mnet's M Countdown with the track "No More Dream" from their debut single album 2 Cool 4 Skool. He has produced and written lyrics for a variety of tracks on all of BTS' albums.

For BTS' third Korean-language extended play (EP) The Most Beautiful Moment in Life, Pt. 1, Suga released a solo intro entitled "Intro: The Most Beautiful Moment in Life". The rap track's lyrics itself discussed the fears of reaching adulthood at the end of one's adolescent years.

It released on April 17, 2015, and featured an animated music video. Pt. 1's follow up EP, The Most Beautiful Moment in Life, Pt. 2, featured another intro performed by Suga, called "Intro: Never Mind", specifically recounting Suga's teenage years. The song released on November 15, 2015, and additionally served as the intro for BTS' 2016 compilation album The Most Beautiful Moment in Life: Young Forever. Suga did not perform another introductory track for BTS until 2020, where he released "Interlude: Shadow" as part of the album roll out for Map of the Soul: 7.

The interlude is a rap song that references "Intro: O!RUL8,2?" from the 2013 EP of the same name, and discusses BTS' fame, comparing its reality to the celebrity O!RUL8,2? dreamed about. The song released on January 10, along with a music video also referencing the struggles of fame. Tamar Herman of Billboard described it as a "evocative, yet brash track" and noted how the song's sound changes midway through to show "this dichotomy between the relationship of how fame and audiences watching him affects his idea of self".

In addition to performing intros for BTS, Suga released two solo tracks under the group's name. The first, a song entitled "First Love", appeared on BTS' 2016 studio album Wings, is an autobiographical rap track reminiscent of a monologue. On the 2018 compilation album Love Yourself: Answer, Suga released the song "Trivia: Seesaw", which discussed the up-and-down nature of falling in love. That same year, Suga was awarded the fifth-class Hwagwan Order of Cultural Merit as a member of BTS by the President of South Korea along with other members of the group.

In July 2021, he was appointed Special Presidential Envoy for Future Generations and Culture by President Moon Jae-in, along with the other members of BTS, to help "lead the global agenda for future generations, such as sustainable growth" and "expand South Korea's diplomatic efforts and global standing" in the international community.

• Suga Solo work

Suga released a free self-titled mixtape via SoundCloud on August 15, 2016. He decided against releasing the project as a commercial studio album, describing it as the "feeling of being trapped in some sort of framework." On the record, he discussed matters such as his struggles with depression and social phobia. Fuse TV rated it one of the top 20 mixtapes of 2016. The following year, in 2017, Suga composed the song "Wine" for singer Suran, whom he had previously worked with for a single on his mixtape. At Suga's studio, Suran heard a rough draft of "Wine" and asked Suga for the song. The record peaked at number two on the Gaon Digital Chart in South Korea and won best Soul/R&B track of the year at the Melon Music Awards on December 2, 2017.

Suga also received the "Hot Trend Award" for his work on the track. Suga later re-released his mixtape for digital purchase and streaming in February 2018. The reissue reached number three on Billboard's World Albums Chart, number five on the Heatseekers Albums chart, and number 74 on the Top Album Sales chart, in the United States. It also caused Suga's solo alias, Agust D, to reach number 46 on the Emerging Artists chart for the week of March 3.

In January 2019, Suga provided a rap feature on Lee So-ra's single "Song Request". The track was co-written by Suga and Tablo of Epik High, who also produced the track. The single debuted at number three on the Gaon

Digital Chart and at number two on Billboard's World Digital Song Sales chart, with 3,000 downloads during the song's two-day charting period. Suga later produced a track for Epik High's Sleepless in extended play, titled "Eternal Sunshine", in February. He co-wrote and produced the digital single, "We Don't Talk Together", for singer Heize, which she released on July 7. In December, American singer-songwriter Halsey released the song "Suga's Interlude", from her third studio album Manic, which both featured and was produced by Suga.

On May 6, 2020, IU released the digital single "Eight" featuring and produced by Suga. The song debuted at number one on both the Gaon Digital Chart and the World Digital Song Sales chart. Suga released his second mixtape, D-2 (the continuation to Agust D), together with the music video for its lead single "Daechwita" on May 22, which peaked at number 76 on the US Billboard Hot 100 chart. The mixtape debuted at number 11 on the Billboard 200 and became the highest-charting album by a Korean soloist in the US. It is also the first Korean solo release to reach the top 10 in the United Kingdom, opening at number seven on the UK albums chart.

In 2021, Suga recomposed Samsung's signature ringtone, "Over The Horizon". The track was unveiled on August 11, as part of Samsung's "Unpacked 2021" event. Suga later produced the single "You" for Japanese singer ØMI, which was released on October 15. In December, Suga featured on the single "Girl of My Dreams" for American rapper Juice Wrld's posthumous album Fighting Demons. The song debuted at number 29 on the Billboard Hot 100, earning Suga his second entry on the chart, as a solo artist.] On April 25, 2022, Suga was revealed as the producer of the lead single "That That" from Psy's album Psy 9th. He also co-wrote and featured on the single, and appeared in the music video alongside Psy.

- Suga Name

Suga at the 2016 Gaon Chart Awards on February 17, 2016.
The stage name Suga is derived from the first syllables of the term shooting guard, the position he played in basketball as a student. He adopted the alias Agust D in 2016 for his mixtape, which is derived from the initials DT, short for his birthplace, Daegu Town, and "Suga" spelled backwards.

- Artistry

Suga writes, composes, arranges, mixes, and masters his own material. Over 100 registered songs are credited to him by the Korea Music Copyright Association. He plays piano and produces mainly hip hop and R&B music. His lyrics involve themes that are "full of dreams and hope," conceived with the intent of his music becoming "many people's strength." He cites Stony Skunk and Epik High as his inspirations to pursue hip hop music. Particularly, he credits the former's reggae-hip hop hybrid album Ragga Muffin (2005) and its title track for igniting his interest in the genre.

Jeff Benjamin of Fuse said that Suga's mixtape "showcases the star's ear for hot productions, hardcore rap style, and how he can make his vulnerabilities a strength." Other critics stated that Suga's "storytelling execution in the music he creates tears down the barrier of censoring and sugarcoating".

In January 2018, Suga was promoted to a full member of the Korea Music Copyright Association.

FOUR

J-HOPE

- *J-Hope*

Jung Ho-seok (born February 18, 1994), better known by his stage name J-Hope (stylized as j-hope), is a South Korean rapper, singer-songwriter, dancer, and record producer. He made his debut as a member of South Korean boy band BTS in 2013, under Big Hit Entertainment.

J-Hope released his first solo mixtape, Hope World, in 2018. The album was met with a positive reception from critics, and peaked at number 38 on the Billboard 200 in the United States, making him the highest-charting solo Korean artist on the ranking at the time. He became the first member of BTS to enter the Billboard Hot 100 as a soloist in 2019, when his single "Chicken Noodle Soup", featuring singer Becky G, debuted at number 81 on the chart. In 2022, J-Hope released his debut studio album Jack in the Box.

- J-Hope life and education

J-Hope was born as Jung Ho-seok on February 18, 1994, in Gwangju, South Korea, where he lived with his parents and older sister, Jung Ji-woo.In March 2019, J-Hope enrolled at Hanyang Cyber University for the Master of Business Administration program in Advertising and Media. He previously graduated from Global Cyber University with a degree in Broadcasting and Entertainment.

- J-Hope Career

Before debuting with BTS, J-Hope was part of an underground dance team called Neuron, and took dance classes at Gwangju Music Academy for six years, from fourth grade to his first year in high school when he signed with Big Hit Entertainment. He was relatively well known for his dance skills, and won various local prizes, including first place in a national dance competition in 2008. His dancing eventually led to an interest in singing, and he auditioned to become an idol trainee. While a trainee, J-Hope appeared as a featured rapper on singer Jo Kwon's song "Animal", released in 2012.

• J-Hope BTS

On June 13, 2013, J-Hope made his debut as a member of BTS on M! Countdown. He was the third member to join the group as a trainee after RM and Suga. On June 14, 2019, J-Hope, together with fellow BTS member V, collaborated with Zara Larsson on a soundtrack called A Brand New Day for a mobile game BTS World.

• J-Hope Solo

J-Hope released his first solo mixtape, Hope World, worldwide on March 1, 2018. It was accompanied by a music video for the lead single "Daydream". A music video for the B-side single "Airplane" was released on March 6. The mixtape debuted at number 63 and peaked at number 38 on the Billboard 200, making him the highest-charting Korean solo act on the ranking up to that point. Six of the album's tracks entered the World Digital Song Sales chart, including "Daydream", which peaked atop the chart, making J-Hope one of only ten Korean artists, including BTS, to reach number one.

The success of his solo debut led to him ranking at number three on the Emerging Artists chart and number 97 on the Artist 100, both for the week of March 10—he peaked at number 91 on the latter the following week. He is the fifth Korean artist, and the second Korean soloist after Psy, to place on the Artist 100. The mixtape charted in ten countries worldwide, with "Daydream" charting in three. It ranked at number five on Billboard's year-end World Albums Chart for 2018. For Hope World's three-year anniversary, J-Hope released the full version of its closing track "Blue Side (Outro)". The three-minute long version was uploaded to the BTS SoundCloud page for free on March 1, 2021.

In 2019, J-Hope released a free collaboration single, "Chicken Noodle Soup", on September 27, featuring American singer Becky G. The track debuted at number 81 on the Billboard Hot 100, making J-Hope the first member of BTS to chart on the Hot 100 as a solo artist outside of the group, the third Korean solo artist to rank on the chart (after Psy and CL), and the sixth Korean artist overall to do so. "Chicken Noodle Soup" also became J-Hope's second song to debut at number one on the World Digital Song Sales chart.

On June 14, 2022, Hybe announced J-Hope as the first member of BTS to begin promotions as a solo artist. His debut solo album Jack in the Box, released on July 15, was preceded by the lead single "More" on July 1. J-Hope made his performance debut at Lollapalooza on July 31, as the headlining act for the final day of the festival. He is the first South Korean artist to headline a main stage at a major United States music festival.

- J-Hope Name

J-Hope performing at the Seoul Olympic Stadium in August 2018, during the Love Yourself World Tour

His stage name, J-Hope, comes from his desire to represent hope for fans, as well as to be "the hope of BTS". It is also a reference to the myth of Pandora's box, as after the box was opened and all the evils inside were released to the world, the only thing left was hope.

J-Hope has been described as having an upbeat and energetic tone to his music and performances. His mixtape, Hope World, was described as having a fun nature and variety of musical genres, including synth-pop, trap, house, alternative hip hop, funk-soul, and retro elements. In a review published by The 405, Emmad Usmani praised the mixtape's concept and production, writing "J-Hope showcases exceptional creativity, genuine personality, and a cohesive sense of direction over the 20 minutes of the project".

Jeff Benjamin of Fuse wrote that the atmospheric style of "Blue Side", Hope World's outro track, "leaves the listener curious for what's coming next from J-Hope". The lyrical elements of the mixtape, notably the lead song "Daydream", was praised by Billboard magazine for its discussion of the difficulties an idol faces in their career, various literary references, and fun presentation of the serious subject matter.

J-Hope cites the adventurous nature of Jules Verne's Twenty Thousand Leagues Under the Sea and the works of Kyle, Aminé, and Joey Badass as influencers on his style and work on Hope World. The idea of peace has also provided a basis for much of his lyrics, stating that "it'd be fantastic to become a part of someone's personal peace through my music" in an interview with Time magazine. The idea of "representing the modern generation" has also influenced his work on BTS' music. There was also a reference to Douglas Adams' science fiction series The Hitchhiker's Guide to the Galaxy.

In 2018, he was awarded the fifth-class Hwagwan Order of Cultural Merit by the President of South Korea along with the other members of the group. He had the most liked tweet in the world for 2018 when he posted the "In My Feelings Challenge".

In July 2021, he was appointed Special Presidential Envoy for Future Generations and Culture by President Moon Jae-in, along with the other members of BTS, to help "lead the global agenda for future generations, such as sustainable growth" and "expand South Korea's diplomatic efforts and global standing" in the international community.

· J-Hope Personal life

In 2016, J-Hope purchased an apartment in South Korea worth US$1.6 million for his personal use. As of 2018, he lives in Hannam-dong, Seoul, South Korea with his bandmates.

J-Hope has been a member of the "Green Noble Club", which recognizes high-value donors of Child Fund Korea, since 2018. On February 18, 2019, he donated 100 million (US$90,000) to the organization in support of those attending his high school alma mater in Gwangju. He previously donated 150 million ($135,000) in December 2018, but requested the donation be kept private at the time.

In December 2019, he donated another 100 million. On November 17, 2020, he donated 100 million in support of children experiencing economic difficulties amid the COVID-19 pandemic. On February 18, 2021, he donated 150 million to support children with visual and hearing impairments. On May 4, for Children's Day, he donated 100 million for children affected by violence in Tanzania, Africa. In December, he donated another 100 million, to cover heating expenses for children in low-income families and childcare facilities, and for medical expenses of pediatric patients. J-Hope has donated a cumulative total of 800 million to Child Fund Korea since 2018.On August 18, 2022, J-Hope donated 100 million to help those affected by the 2022 South

Korean floods through the Hope Bridge Korea Disaster Relief Association.

FIVE
RM (RAPPER)

- *RM (rapper)*

Kim Nam-joon (born September 12, 1994), known professionally as RM (formerly Rap Monster), is a South Korean rapper, singer-songwriter and record producer. He is the leader of the South Korean boy group BTS.

RM released his first solo mixtape, RM, in 2015. In 2018, he released his second mixtape, Mono, which peaked at number 26 on the US Billboard 200 and became the highest-charting album by a Korean soloist in chart history. He has also collaborated with artists such as Wale, Younha, Warren G, Gaeko, Krizz Kaliko, MFBTY, Fall Out Boy, Primary, and Lil Nas X.

- RM (rapper) life and education

Kim Nam-joon was born on September 12, 1994, in Dongjak District, Seoul, South Korea and grew up in Ilsan District, Goyang, where his family moved when he was aged four or five. The elder of two siblings, he has a younger sister. As a child, RM largely learned English by watching the American sitcom Friends with his mother. As a student, he actively wrote poetry and often received awards for his writing. He posted his work to an online poetry website for roughly one year, where he received moderate attention. As a result, RM expressed interest in pursuing a literary career but later decided against it. When he was twelve years old, he studied in New Zealand for four months.

At age 11, in fifth grade, RM became interested in hip-hop music after hearing Epik High's "Fly". Finding that the song had provided him comfort, he decided to look further into the genre. He was introduced to the music of American rapper Eminem by his school teacher, which first sparked RM's interest in lyricism. He would print out lyrics that he felt were "cool" and shared them with friends. RM began songwriting at that time, stating that his poetry became lyrics when it combined with music. In 2007, as a first-year middle school student, he began rapping in local amateur hip-hop circles, creating his first self-composed recording with the program Adobe Audition and later participating in his first concert in 2008.RM became more active in the underground Korean hip-hop scene under the moniker Runch Randa, releasing a number of tracks and collaborations with other underground rappers such as Zico.

In school, RM had an IQ of 148 and scored in the top 1% of the nation in the university entrance examinations for language, math, foreign language and social studies.Because his parents had been strongly opposed to his interest in a musical career due to his academic achievements, RM initially decided to set music aside to focus on his studies. He eventually convinced his mother to allow him to be a rapper, asking her if "she wanted to have a son who was a first-place rapper, or a 5,000th-place student".

In March 2019, after graduating from Global Cyber University with a degree in Broadcasting and Entertainment, RM enrolled at Hanyang Cyber University's Master of Business Administration program in Advertising and Media.

• RM (rapper) Name

RM selected the name "Rap Monster" during his time as an idol trainee. The name derives from the lyrics of a song he wrote, inspired by San E's "Rap Genius". The lyrics contained a segment where San E declares he should be called a "rap monster" as he "raps non-stop". He adopted the stage name because he felt it was "cool". RM has described himself as having a love-hate relationship with the name, feeling that it was not selected for being of "incredible value" to him.

He formally changed his stage name to "RM" in November 2017, as he determined that "Rap Monster" was no longer representative of who he was or the music that he creates. In an interview with Entertainment Tonight in 2019, RM stated that the name "could symbolize many things" and "could have more spectrums to it." One meaning that has been suggested is "Real Me".

- RM (rapper) Career

In 2009, RM auditioned for Big Deal Records, passing the first round along with Samuel Seo but failing the second round after forgetting lyrics. However, following the audition, rapper Sleepy exchanged contact information with RM, whom he later mentioned to Big Hit Entertainment producer Pdogg. In 2010, Sleepy contacted RM, encouraging him to audition for Big Hit Entertainment CEO Bang Si-hyuk. Bang offered RM, then aged 16, a spot at the record label, which he accepted immediately and without his parents' knowledge. Bang and Pdogg soon began forming a hip hop group that would eventually become the idol group BTS.

RM trained for three years with fellow rapper Min Yoon-gi and dancer Jung Ho-seok, later known as Suga and J-Hope, respectively. During this three-year trainee period, RM performed on five pre-debut tracks credited to BTS in 2010 and 2011.

He also worked as a songwriter for girl group Glam and helped pen their debut single "Party (XXO)", a pro-LGBTQ song that was praised by Billboard as "one of the most forward-thinking songs out of a K-pop girl group in the past decade." On June 13, 2013, RM made his debut with BTS and has since produced and written lyrics for many tracks on their albums. On August 29, 2013, RM performed the intro track to BTS' first extended play (EP), which was released as a trailer ahead of the EP's September 11 release, marking his first solo after debuting.

- RM performing with BTS

On August 5, 2014, Big Hit Entertainment released a trailer for BTS' first studio album Dark & Wild, which was set to be released on August 20. The rap track, officially credited to BTS as "Intro: What Am I to You?", was a solo performed by RM. Through reality television show American Hustle Life, which was used to produce Dark & Wild, RM formed a working relationship with Warren G, who offered to write BTS a beat. In an interview with Korean magazine Hip Hop Playa, Warren G stated that he had befriended BTS through the program and had kept in touch with the band after they returned to South Korea. On March 4, 2015, RM released a single with Warren G entitled, "P.D.D (Please Don't Die)" ahead of his first solo mixtape RM following an offer by Warren G to collaborate.

The track reflected how RM felt towards those who hated and criticized him at the time, which he used to find very upsetting. That same March, RM collaborated with hip hop project group MFBTY, EE and Dino J on the song "Bucku Bucku". He featured in the song's music video and also had a cameo appearance in a music video for another song by MFBTY, "Bang Diggy Bang Bang". RM had first formed a lasting working relationship with MFBTY member Tiger JK after meeting and expressing admiration for him on a TV show in 2013, when Tiger JK was promoting his song "The Cure".

RM was cast as a regular on the Korean variety program Problematic Men, where cast members were given a variety of puzzles and problems to solve and work through by discussing their own thoughts and experiences. The program began airing on February 26, 2015; however, RM left the show after 22 episodes due to BTS' 2015 Red Bullet world tour.

On March 17, 2015, RM released his first solo mixtape, RM, which ranked 48th on Spin's "50 Best Hip Hop Albums of 2015". The mixtape addressed a variety of topics, such as RM's past on the track "Voice" and the idea that "you're you and I'm me" in the track "Do You". When discussing the track "God Rap", RM described himself as an atheist, believing that only he could determine his fate. The production process for the mixtape lasted around four or five months, with RM working on it in between BTS' activities.

The following year, RM recalled that he had largely written about the negative emotions he had been carrying, such as anger and rage, but stated that the songs are not "100% under [his] sovereignty" and that he felt many parts of the mixtape were "immature". He also added that he hoped his next mixtape to be something he worked on by himself. Following RM's release, he featured along with Kwon Jin-ah on Primary's "U" that April. In August, RM collaborated with Marvel for Fantastic Four's soundtrack in Korea, releasing the digital single, "Fantastic" featuring Mandy Ventrice through Melon, Genie, Naver Music and other music platforms. In August 2016, vocal duo Homme released a single titled "Dilemma", which was co-produced by RM and Bang Si-hyuk.

In March 2017, RM collaborated with American rapper Wale on a special socially-charged track called "Change", released as a free digital download along with an accompanying music video filmed two weeks prior to the track's release. The pair first formed a relationship over Twitter, with Wale reaching out to RM in 2016, having seen RM's cover of his track "Illest Bitch". RM decided on the topic of "Change", saying that though the two rappers were extremely different, their commonality lay in the fact that both America and South Korea had their political and social situations and that both of them wanted the world to change for the better. One month later, RM featured on the track "Gajah" with Gaeko of Dynamic Duo. In December, RM collaborated on a remix of Fall Out Boy's song "Champion". The track reached number 18 on Billboard's Bubbling Under Hot 100 Singles and helped RM reach number 46 on the Emerging Artists Chart for the week of January 8, 2018. On December 27, RM made history as the first K-pop artist to chart on the Rock Digital Songs chart, placing at number two.

RM released his second mixtape, Mono, which he referred to as a "playlist", on October 23, 2018. He became the first Korean artist to rank number one on the Emerging Artists Chart in the United States with its release. The playlist was well-received by critics, who praised RM for laying "his deep insecurities bare on songs like 'Tokyo' and 'Seoul'". The track "Seoul" was produced by British electropop duo Honne, who first discovered RM after seeing him recommend their music on Twitter and eventually met him in Seoul following one of their concerts. In November, RM also collaborated with Tiger JK on his last and final album under the stage name Drunken Tiger, featuring on the track "Timeless". Tiger JK originally expected RM's lyrics to contain self-praise, which was the trend of rap at the time; RM instead wrote lyrics about leaving behind the historical meaning of Drunken Tiger's name.

On March 25, 2019, Honne announced that RM would feature on their remake of "Crying Over You" alongside singer BEKA, which was released on March 27. Honne originally released "Crying Over You" with BEKA in 2018. The song was originally slated for a January 2019 release but postponed due to "unforeseen circumstances".Chinese singer Bibi Zhou was added to the Chinese release, appearing with RM and replacing BEKA.The same day, Big Hit Entertainment released the song "Persona" as a trailer for BTS' EP Map of the Soul: Persona, performed as a solo by RM. Persona debuted at number 17 on Billboard's YouTube Song Chart. Three months later, on July 24, 2019, RM featured on the fourth official remix of Lil Nas X's "Old Town Road," entitled "Seoul Town Road", in which he "infuse his English-language verse with a surprisingly good Southern twang". On December 29, it was announced that RM would feature on Younha's track "Winter Flower", released on January 6, 2020. RM also featured on "Don't", the lead single of Korean singer eAeon's second solo album released on April 30, 2021.

- Artistry and impact

RM is a baritone. In 2017, American hip-hop magazine XXL included him in its list of "10 Korean Rappers You Should Know", with writer Peter A. Berry stating that "Rap Monster rarely fails to live up to his name". Berry described RM as "one of the region's most dexterous rappers, capable of switching flows effortlessly as he glides across an array of diverse instrumentals". Crystal Tai of the South China Morning Post noted that RM has "received much praise for his natural flow and lyrics". Speaking about RM's work, Noisey's Bianca Mendez wrote that "he's got some My Beautiful Dark Twisted Fantasy in him, but he's closer to...Earl Sweatshirt and Chance the Rapper in spirit, and that's exciting". In January 2020, he was promoted from associate to a full member of the Korea Music Copyright Association.

In a survey conducted by Gallup Korea, RM ranked as the 12th most preferred idol of the year for 2018. He ranked 11th in 2019. In 2018, RM was awarded the fifth-class Hwagwan Order of Cultural Merit by the President of South Korea, along with the other members of BTS, for his contributions to spreading Korean culture. In July 2021, he and the members of BTS were appointed Special Presidential Envoy for Future Generations and Culture by President Moon Jae-in to help "lead the global agenda for future generations, such as sustainable growth" and "expand South Korea's diplomatic efforts and global standing" in the international community.

SIX

JIMIN

◦─────♭─────◦

- *Jimin*

Park Ji-min (born October 13, 1995), known mononymously as Jimin, is a South Korean singer and dancer. In 2013, he made his debut as a member of the South Korean boy group BTS, under the record label Big Hit Entertainment.

Jimin has released three solo tracks with BTS: "Lie" in 2016, "Serendipity" in 2017, and "Filter" in 2020, all of which have charted on South Korea's Gaon Digital Chart. In 2018, he released his first independent song, the digital track "Promise", which he co-wrote and co-composed. He appeared on the soundtrack for the 2022 TvN drama Our Blues, and sang "With You", a duet with Ha Sung-woon.

- Jimin life and education

Park Ji-min was born on October 13, 1995, in Geumjeong District, Busan, South Korea. His immediate family includes his mother, father, and younger brother. When he was a child, he attended Busan's Hodong Elementary School and Yonsan Middle School. During middle school, he attended Just Dance Academy and learned popping and locking dance. Prior to becoming a trainee, Jimin studied contemporary dance at Busan High School of Arts and was a top student in the modern dance department. After a teacher suggested he audition with an entertainment company, it led him to Big Hit Entertainment. Once he passed the auditions in 2012, he transferred to Korean Arts High School, graduating in 2014.

Jimin graduated from Global Cyber University in August 2020, with a major in Broadcasting and Entertainment. As of 2021, he is enrolled at Hanyang Cyber University, pursuing a Master of Business Administration in Advertising and Media.

- Jimin performing at Incheon Sky

Jimin debuted as a member of BTS on June 13, 2013, and holds the position of vocalist and dancer in the group. Under BTS, he has released three solo songs: "Lie", "Serendipity", and "Filter". "Lie" was released in 2016, as part of the group's second Korean studio album, Wings. It was described as stunning and dramatic, conveying dark undertones and emotions that helped reflect the overall concept of the album. In contrast, "Serendipity", released on the Love Yourself: Her (2017) extended play (EP), was soft and sensual, unraveling the joy, conviction, and curiosity of love. "Filter", from the group's 2020 studio album, Map of the Soul: 7, was very different from its predecessor, with a distinct Latin pop-esque flair and lyrics that reflected on the different sides of himself that Jimin shows to the world and those around him.

"Serendipity" and "Lie" both surpassed fifty million streams on Spotify in 2018, followed shortly thereafter by the former's full length version from BTS' Love Yourself: Answer (2018) compilation album, which achieved the milestone in early 2019. With this, Jimin set a new record as the only Korean artist to have three solo tracks accumulate over 50 million streams each—previously Psy was the only Korean artist to cross the 50 million streams mark with "Gangnam Style" (2012) and "Gentleman" (2013). Both songs were also the only solos by a BTS member included in the Official Chart Company's list of the top 20 most streamed BTS songs in the United Kingdom as of October 2018, ranking at number 17 and 19 respectively. In April 2019, the list was expanded to reflect the top 40, and both tracks were the highest ranked solo songs included that year, at numbers 18 and 20 respectively.

In May 2019, Jimin became the first BTS member to have a solo music video achieve 100 million views on YouTube when "Serendipity" achieved the milestone. He was the only BTS member with multiple solo songs in the January 2020 update of the Official Chart's top 40 list. "Lie" and "Serendipity" were the second and third most-streamed solos, at numbers 24 and 29 respectively, with the full length version of the latter debuting at number 38.

In February, "Filter" set a record for the biggest streaming debut among all Korean songs on Spotify with over 2.2 million streams in its first 24 hours of release, and went on to become the fastest Korean solo in the platform's history to surpass 20–60 million streams. It is also the only solo BTS b-side track to receive a Song of The Year nomination at the Gaon Chart Music Awards. In March 2021, it became the 15th BTS song to spend a full year on Billboard's World Digital Song Sales chart. It is the longest-charting Korean song released in 2020 on the World ranking, having spent 80 weeks on the chart as of the issue dated October 9, 2021.

Jimin was awarded the fifth-class Hwagwan Order of Cultural Merit in 2018 by the President of South Korea, Moon Jae-in, alongside the other members of BTS for their contributions to the promotion of Korean culture. In July 2021, President Moon appointed him Special Presidential Envoy for Future Generations and Culture, along with the other members of BTS, to help "lead the global agenda for future generations, such as sustainable growth" and "expand South Korea's diplomatic efforts and global standing" in the international community.

· Jimin on the set of the "Boy with Luv"

In 2014, Jimin collaborated with bandmate and fellow vocalist Jungkook on a song called "Christmas Day", a Korean rendition of Justin Bieber's "Mistletoe"—he wrote the Korean lyrics himself. The two collaborated again in 2017, for a cover of American singer Charlie Puth's "We Don't Talk Anymore" (2016)—Jimin sang the parts of Selena Gomez who featured on the original with Puth. Jungkook had previously released a solo version of the song earlier that year in February, and the two prepared the duet as a special gift to the band's fandom, releasing it on June 2 during BTS' fourth anniversary celebrations. Commenting on Jimin's appearance on the track, Teen Vogue wrote that "adding Jimin's voice to the mix makes the rendition all the more lovely". Canadian outlet Flare magazine also praised his rendition saying, "...no shade, Selena—it honestly might be better than the original". Elite Daily described the cover as "nothing short of flawless".

Jimin appeared on several variety shows such as Hello Counselor, Please Take Care of My Refrigerator, and God's Workplace in 2016. He also served as a special MC on domestic television music programs such as Show! Music Core and M Countdown. In December 2016, he participated in a dance duet at the KBS Song Festival with Taemin from Shinee.

On December 30, 2018, Jimin released his first solo song outside of BTS releases, "Promise", for free on BTS' SoundCloud page. On January 3, 2019, the platform announced that "Promise" had surpassed the record set by Drake's "Duppy Freestyle" for the biggest 24-hour debut in history. Described by Billboard as a "mellow pop ballad",the song was composed by Jimin and Big Hit producer Slow Rabbit, who also produced the track, and features lyrics written by Jimin and bandmate RM. On December 24, 2020, he released his second solo song "Christmas Love", a song about his childhood memories of the holidays. In 2022, Jimin participated in the soundtrack for the TvN drama Our Blues, the first television OST of his career. Titled "With You", the single is a duet with Ha Sung-woon and was released on April 24.

- Jimin performing "Blood Sweat & Tears" at the 2016 Melon Music Awards.

Jimin's vocals have been described as delicate and sweet. He is regarded as an exceptional dancer among the members of the group and in K-pop in general. Noelle Devoe of Elite Daily wrote that he is often praised for his "smooth and elegant movements" as well as his charm on stage. In the BTS documentary Burn the Stage, Jimin said he thinks of himself as a perfectionist and that even the smallest mistakes on stage make him feel guilty and stressed.

He has cited singer Rain as one of his inspirations and reasons why he wanted to become both a singer and performer.

In 2016, Jimin was ranked as the 14th most popular idol in an annual survey conducted by Gallup Korea. He subsequently ranked seventh in 2017, and then consecutively ranked first in 2018 and 2019, as the only idol to top the survey for two consecutive years. In 2018, Jimin was the ninth most-tweeted about celebrity and the eighth most-tweeted about musician globally. He was picked as the 17th best boyband member in history by The Guardian. From January to May 2018, Jimin won the monthly Peeper x Billboard Award for "Top K-Pop Artist–Individual". Peeper x Billboard is a collaboration between the Peeper social media app and Billboard Korea that collects fan votes for their favorite K-pop artists and announces monthly winners. The prize was a donation to UNICEF in his name.

The Cultural Conservation Society awarded Jimin a plaque of appreciation in 2019, for performing buchaechum, a traditional Korean fan dance, during the 2018 Melon Music Awards and helping spread the dance outside of Korea. In October 2021, he became the first idol to spend 34 consecutive months atop the brand reputation ranking for individual boy group idols, and is the only idol to top the overall ranking for three consecutive years.

Jimin is often cited as an influence or role model by various idols in the K-pop industry, many of whom try to emulate his style of dance, mannerisms, and stage presence. This has earned him the titles "Idol of Idols", "Idol's Bible", and "Rookies' Bible", from news and entertainment media. Some idols who have named him include Arthur of Kingdom, MCND's Bic, BDC's Kim Si-hun, Newkidd's Woochul, Stray Kids' Hyunjin, Wooyoung of Ateez, Victon's Lim Se-jun, Huening Kai and Beomgyu from TXT, and Enhypen's Ni-ki and Jay. Oli London, a British influencer, underwent 18 surgeries costing up to £150,000 to look like him.

· Philanthropy

From 2016 to 2018, Jimin supported graduates of his alma mater, Busan Hodong Elementary School, by covering uniform expenses. After news of the school's closing was released, he donated summer and winter middle school uniforms to the final graduates and gifted autographed albums to the entire student body. In early 2019, Jimin donated KRW100 million (US$88,000) to the Busan Department of Education to help support lower income students. Of the total, 30 million ($23,000) went to his alma mater, Busan Arts High School. In July 2020, he donated another 100 million, this time to the Jeonnam Future Education Foundation, for the creation of a scholarship fund for talented but financially struggling students from South Jeolla Province.

In July 2021, Jimin donated 100 million to Rotary International, to help polio patients. As with previous donations, the benefaction was made privately, but the news became public in September, when the Go-seong Rotary Club displayed a banner thanking him for the donation. On October 12, 2021, he was announced as a member of the Green Noble Club, a group of major donors to the Green Umbrella Children's Foundation who have made donations of 100 million or more.

Since 2018, Jimin has lived in Hannam-dong, Seoul, South Korea, with his bandmates. In 2021, he purchased a property in the area, worth US$5.3 million.

SEVEN

JUNGKOOK

- *Jungkook*

Jeon Jung-kook (born September 1, 1997), known mononymously as Jungkook, is a South Korean singer and songwriter. He is the youngest member and vocalist of the South Korean boy band BTS.

Jungkook has released three solo tracks with BTS: "Begin" in 2016, "Euphoria" in 2018, and "My Time" in 2020, all of which have charted on South Korea's Gaon Digital Chart. He also sang the soundtrack for the BTS-based webtoon 7Fates: Chakho, titled "Stay Alive". In 2022, he was featured on the single "Left and Right" by American singer-songwriter Charlie Puth, which peaked at number 22 on the U.S. Billboard Hot 100.

- Jungkook life and education

Jeon Jung-kook was born on September 1, 1997, in Busan, South Korea. His family consists of his parents and an elder brother. He attended Baekyang Elementary and Middle School in Busan. When he became a trainee, he transferred to Singu Middle School in Seoul. Jungkook initially had dreams of becoming a badminton player when he was younger, but after seeing G-Dragon perform "Heartbreaker" on television, it influenced him to want to become a singer.

In 2011, Jungkook auditioned for the South Korean talent show Superstar K during its auditions in Daegu. Though he was not selected, he received casting offers from seven entertainment companies. He eventually chose to become a trainee under Big Hit Entertainment after seeing RM, now his fellow band member and leader in BTS, perform. To work on his dance skills in preparation for debut, he went to Los Angeles during the summer of 2012 to receive dance training from Movement Lifestyle. In June 2012, he appeared in Jo Kwon's "I'm Da One" music video and also worked as a backup dancer for Glam before his debut.

He graduated from School of Performing Arts Seoul, an arts high school, in 2017. In November 2016, he decided to forgo taking the CSATs, Korea's nationwide university entrance exam. In March 2022, he received his degree from Global Cyber University's Department of Broadcasting and Entertainment. He was awarded with the President's Award, the school's highest honor.

• Jungkook Career & Jungkook performing

On June 12, 2013, Jungkook made his debut as a member of BTS with the release of the single 2 Cool 4 Skool. Under BTS, he has sung three solo songs; the first, pop track "Begin" from the 2016 album Wings, told his story of moving to Seoul at a young age to become an idol and expresses his gratitude towards his fellow members for taking care of him during that time.

The second, a future bass song titled "Euphoria", was released with an accompanying nine-minute short film on April 5, 2018, as the introduction to the third part of BTS' "Love Yourself" series. Produced by DJ Swivel, the song charted at number five on the Billboard Bubbling Under Hot 100. Its full studio version was included on BTS' Love Yourself: Answer compilation album, released on August 24.

The third solo, "My Time", off the band's 2020 studio album Map of the Soul: 7, is a strobing R&B song about forgoing teenage experiences because of his career, and charted at number 84 on the US Billboard Hot 100. "Euphoria" and "My Time" are the first and second longest-charting solo tracks among K-pop singers on the Billboard World Digital Song Sales chart, having spent a record 90 and 85 weeks respectively on the ranking.

Jungkook has been credited as the main producer for two of BTS' songs: "Love is Not Over" and "Magic Shop".

On October 25, 2018, Jungkook (together with the rest of the BTS members) was ordained with the fifth-class Hwagwan Order of Cultural Merit by the President of South Korea. In July 2021, he was appointed Special Presidential Envoy for Future Generations and Culture by President Moon

Jae-in, along with the other members of BTS, to help "lead the global agenda for future generations, such as sustainable growth" and "expand South Korea's diplomatic efforts and global standing" in the international community.

• Jungkook performing "Boy With Luv"

In September 2015, Jungkook participated in the "One Dream, One Korea" campaign, taking part in a song collaboration alongside numerous Korean artists in memory of the Korean War. The song was released September 24 and presented at the One K Concert in Seoul on October 15.In 2016, Jungkook was cast in the pilot episode of Flower Crew. He also appeared on Celebrity Bromance, and competed in King of Mask Singer under the name "Fencing Man," appearing in episode 72.

On November 6, 2018, Jungkook performed "We Don't Talk Anymore" with original singer Charlie Puth in a special collaboration stage during the MBC Plus X Genie Music Awards. The song was one he had previously covered twice, solo and with fellow BTS member Jimin.

On June 4, 2020, Jungkook released the song "Still With You", for free on platforms such as SoundCloud as a part of BTS' yearly debut celebrations. Billboard described the song as having "tinkling synths and gently strummed guitars and brushed drums". Jungkook produced the piece himself.

In February 2022, Jungkook sang the soundtrack for 7Fates: Chakho, a new BTS-based webtoon. Titled "Stay Alive", and produced by fellow BTS member Suga, the song earned Jungkook his first solo entry on the Billboard Hot 100 with its debut at number 95, and his first solo top-ten entry on the Billboard Global Excl. U.S chart at number eight. In the UK, it became the first Korean soundtrack in history to debut on the OCC's Official Singles Chart, entering the ranking at number 89. Jungkook collaborated again with Puth, featuring on the single "Left and Right", which was released on June 24.

In a 2019 survey conducted by Gallup Korea, Jungkook ranked as the third most-loved celebrity of the year in South Korea. He debuted on the list in 2016 at 20th, then ranked 17th in 2017, and then 8th in 2018. In 2018, Jungkook placed first for 10 weeks in a row for magazine Hi China, under the most beloved celebrities list in China. Jungkook is also extremely popular on social media amongst fans. In December 2018, a video of him singing in the studio became the most retweeted tweet in South Korea that year.Various artists have cited him as an influence and role model, such as Kim Dong-han and Hyeongseop X Euiwoong. Jungkook has cited Justin Bieber, Justin Timberlake and Usher among his musical inspirations.

Jungkook's popularity has earned him the nickname "Sold Out King" as items that he is seen using often sell out quickly. These include shoes, Downy fabric softener, wine, novels—namely I Decided to Live as Me by Kim Soo-hyun, which became a best-seller in both Korea and Japan—and Hanbok. Korean media reported that Jungkook had created a "Modern Hanbok" fashion trend in the Korean entertainment industry when celebrities such as Jun Hyun-moo, Jang Do-yeon, Gong Hyo-jin, MC Oh Seung-hwan and The Return of Superman's Park Joo-ho began wearing similar clothing after he was photographed wearing it.

Jungkook was 2019's most-searched male K-pop idol on Google according to their mid-year chart. He topped the chart again in 2020, and was the most searched K-pop idol on YouTube in 2019 and 2020. On Tumblr, he ranked 1st in 'Top K-Pop Stars' for 3 consecutive years. On Twitter, he had the most retweeted tweet of 2019, and the 2nd most retweeted tweet of 2020. In March 2021, Jungkook set a new all-time record for the most real-time viewers in V Live history when his solo live broadcast surpassed 22 million simultaneous viewers—he first broke the record in October 2018, when his broadcast surpassed 3.7 million viewers worldwide.

In June 2021, a lawmaker of the Justice Party used photos of him to promote the legalization of tattoos in South Korea, which works under regulations. The posts were widely condemned by netizens, who accused the lawmaker of taking advantage of Jungkook's fame for political purposes. In the same year images of Jungkook were posted by the mayor of Tagbilaran in the Philippines, John Geesnell Yap, to convince citizens to receive the COVID shot.

· Jungkook life

In 2017, Jungkook collapsed during a concert in Chile. It was later revealed that he had been feeling unwell that day and there were no underlying issues. He suffered a heel injury on the Love Yourself World Tour in 2018, preventing him from participating in choreography; as a result, he sang while seated during part the European leg of the tour.

In November 2019, Jungkook was involved in a car accident with a taxi. Neither party had any major injuries and an amicable settlement was agreed upon.Since 2018, Jungkook has lived in Hannam-dong, Seoul, South Korea with his bandmates. In July 2019, he purchased an apartment in Yongsan District, Seoul worth 4 billion, which he gifted to his older brother in December 2020. As of July 2021, Jungkook's net worth was estimated to be US$20 million.